· little tales ·
The Three Little Pigs

This is a Parragon Book
This edition published in 2001

Parragon
Queen Street House
4 Queen Street
Bath BA1 1HE, UK

Produced by
The Templar Company plc,
Pippbrook Mill, London Road,
Dorking, Surrey RH4 1JE.

Cover design by Andrea Newton
Printed in Singapore
ISBN 0-75254-931-6

· little tales ·
The Three
Little Pigs

Retold by Stephanie Laslett
Illustrated by Jenny Press

p

Once upon a time there were three little pigs. They lived at home with their mother in a snug little house close by a babbling brook. The three pigs were very fond of their food, as most pigs are, and soon they had grown up to be big and strong.

Gradually, the snug little house became too small for the three of them.

At meal times they had trouble sitting round the little kitchen table. Most of the time it was a terrible squeeze.

In the bathroom, they had trouble getting their toothbrushes near their teeth. And upstairs in the bedroom, they had trouble getting their trousers over the right trotters!

One day their mother spoke out.

"You are big enough now to find houses of your own," she said. "Take good care of yourselves — and watch out for the big, bad wolf!"

So the three little pigs
set off down the road.

Soon they met a man carrying a large bundle of straw.

"Please may I have some straw to build a house?" asked the first little pig.

"Certainly you may," replied the man.

Straightaway, the pig set to work and in a short while had finished

his very own house, made
entirely of straw. It was
a little shaky — but
very warm and dry.

"The wolf won't catch
me now!" declared the
first little pig proudly.

The other two little

pigs carried on down the road. Soon they met a man carrying a large bundle of sticks.

"Please may I have some sticks to build a house?" asked the second pig.

"Certainly you may," replied the man. Soon the little pig was hard at work and when he was finished, he stood back

and admired his fine new home. It was a little draughty — but it looked good and strong.

"What a fine house," he said. "The wolf certainly won't catch me now!"

The third little pig

walked on down the road and soon met a man carrying a large load of bricks.

"Please may I have some bricks to build a house?" asked the third little pig.

"Certainly you may," replied the man. All day long the pig worked on his house. He mixed

cement, he built thick walls and as the sun went down, he laid his very last brick.

"Excellent!" he said. "The wolf won't catch me now!"

The very next day who

should come calling but
the big bad wolf! Down
the road he prowled,
peering under hedgerows
and pouncing behind
bushes. When he saw
the little straw house,
he was most surprised.

"I wonder who lives here?" he said. And he decided to have a look.

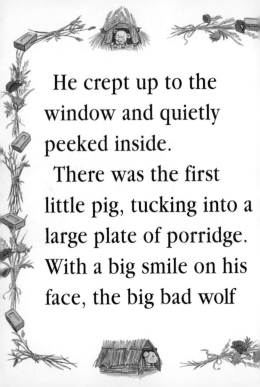

He crept up to the window and quietly peeked inside.

There was the first little pig, tucking into a large plate of porridge. With a big smile on his face, the big bad wolf

knocked gleefully at the
front door.

"Little pig, little·pig,
let me come in," called
the wolf in a growly
voice. The first little pig
dropped his spoon in
fright.

"No, no! By the hair of my chinny chin chin, I will NOT let you in!" he shouted.

"Then I'll puff, and I'll huff, and I'll blow your house in!" shouted the

wolf. The poor little pig trembled and stuffed his trotters in his ears.

Outside, the wolf huffed and he puffed and he puffed and he huffed and he blew the house down. In a trice, he had eaten the first little pig all up. Licking his lips, the big bad wolf set off down the road. Soon he saw a nice little house made all of sticks.

"I wonder who lives here?" said the wolf. He tiptoed up to the window and peeped inside. There was the second little pig, just finishing his third cup of tea.

With a wicked grin, the big bad wolf marched up and knocked loudly at the front door. Rat, tat, tat! he went.

"Little pig, little pig, let me come in," he called. The second little pig jumped in the air, spilling hot tea all over his toast.

"No, no! By the hair on my chinny chin chin, I will NOT let you in!" he shouted.

"Then I'll huff and I'll puff, and I'll blow your house in!" shouted the wolf. The little pig hid under the table. Outside, the wolf laughed. Then he huffed and he puffed and he puffed and he huffed and he blew the house down. In two ticks, he had eaten the second little pig all up.

Patting his stomach, the big bad wolf strolled on down the road. Soon he came upon a smart house made of bricks.

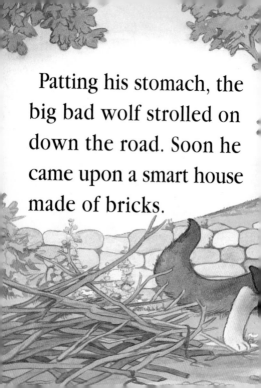

"I wonder who lives in this fine house?" cried the wolf with a wink and a sly smirk. Inside, the third little pig sat back in his comfortable armchair and carried on reading his newspaper.

He wasn't at all bothered
by that silly old wolf.

"Little pig, little pig," the
wolf called softly through
the letterbox. "Little pig,
little pig. Let me come in."

The little pig shook his
newspaper crossly.

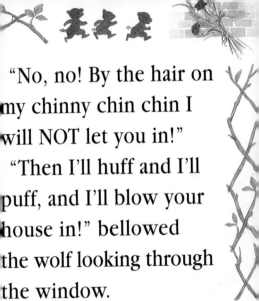

"No, no! By the hair on my chinny chin chin I will NOT let you in!"

"Then I'll huff and I'll puff, and I'll blow your house in!" bellowed the wolf looking through the window.

"Puff away! Huff away!"
replied the pig carelessly.
"You don't scare me!"

The wolf just smiled. He had blown down the house of straw. He had blown down the house of sticks. He was sure he could blow down a house of bricks.

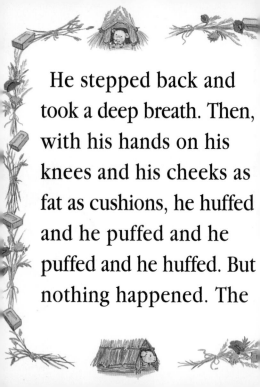

He stepped back and took a deep breath. Then, with his hands on his knees and his cheeks as fat as cushions, he huffed and he puffed and he puffed and he huffed. But nothing happened. The

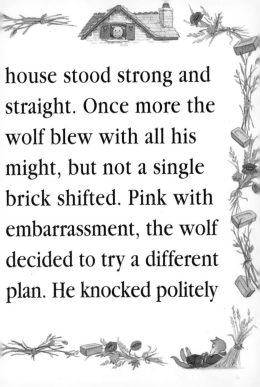

house stood strong and
straight. Once more the
wolf blew with all his
might, but not a single
brick shifted. Pink with
embarrassment, the wolf
decided to try a different
plan. He knocked politely

on the little pig's door.

"Oh, little pig, I hear you like turnips. Well, the best turnips grow in Father Smith's field and if you can be ready at six o'clock in the morning I will take you there."

"I'll be ready," replied
the little pig.

So the next morning at
six o'clock the wolf
came calling at the door.

"Are you ready, little
pig?" he cried.

"Ready?" replied the pig.

"I was ready long ago. I have already fetched my turnips and now they are cooking in my pot!"

The wolf turned red with anger. He could smell a delicious aroma wafting from the little

pig's chimney. Slowly
the wolf counted to ten
and tried to calm himself.
He had another plan.

"Oh, little pig. I know you like apples. Well, tomorrow morning at five o'clock I am going to Merrygarden Farm to pick as many as I like. If you can be ready you can come with me."

"I'll be ready," replied the little pig.

The next morning the little pig left his house at four o'clock to be sure to beat the wolf — but he wasn't quick enough! He was high up an apple tree, eating his fill, when the big bad wolf arrived.

"Ah, there you are," called the wolf. "Are the apples good?" The pig nearly fell out of the tree in fright. The wolf had him trapped! How he wished he was safe at home inside his strong house of bricks. Slowly the wolf prowled around the trunk, never taking his eyes off the pig for a second. Then the little pig had a clever idea.

"Those really are very tasty apples, Mr. Wolf,"

he called down. "Surely
you would like to try
one?"

And he threw an apple as far as he could across the orchard.

The greedy wolf went bounding after it and, in a flash, the pig was down the tree and running for home, licketty-spit.

The wolf turned purple with rage, but was determined not to be

beaten by the clever
little pig. He called at
the house the next day.
"I am going to the fair
this afternoon. Would
you like to come with
me?" he asked, in as
friendly a voice as he

could manage. The little pig looked out through his letterbox.

76

"Another trick!" thought the little pig. "Well, I got to the turnips before him. I got to the apples before him. I'm sure I will be able to get to the fair before him," and so the little pig agreed to meet the wolf at three o'clock. But at two o'clock the pig set off on his own. He had a lovely time at the fair and bought a beautiful big butter churn. On his way home he spied the wolf

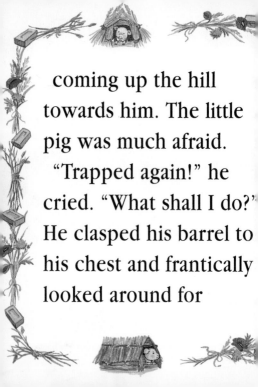

coming up the hill towards him. The little pig was much afraid.

"Trapped again!" he cried. "What shall I do?" He clasped his barrel to his chest and frantically looked around for

somewhere to hide. But the fields stretched out on all sides without so much as a thorn bush or a holly hedge to give him cover. Then the pig looked at his butter churn and laughed.

"This will save me," he chuckled and into the barrel he jumped. It rolled down the road, faster and faster.

It frightened the wolf
so much that he nearly
leapt out of his skin!
  The pig rolled on down
the road and soon was
safe and sound at home.
He was just tucking
into his second slice of

apple cake when there was a timid knock at the door.

The pig looked through the window and there stood the wolf, with knees knocking, looking very worried indeed.

"A horrible monster attacked me on the way to the fair," he quavered. The pig thought this was very funny.

"Why, that was me in my butter churn," he laughed.

When the wolf heard this, he nearly exploded.

"Little pig, little pig," he shouted. "I am going to climb down your chimney and eat you all up right now!"

Quickly the pig lit a fire under his large pot of water. As the flames leapt higher and higher, the water bubbled hotter and hotter.

The wolf climbed up to the roof. He made a terrible noise, slipping on the brick tiles.

The little pig listened hard and heard the wolf reach the chimney pot. Clatter, clatter! went the wolf's claws and soon the little pig could hear him squeezing his way down the chimney.

When the little pig saw the end of the wolf's tail, he lifted the lid of his cooking pot. Down came the wolf and with a splash! he fell straight into the boiling water.

Clang! Back went the lid

and soon the wolf was
dead.

But, as I expect you
can guess, the third
little pig lived happily
ever after and was
never troubled by a big
bad wolf again!

J. O. HALLIWELL

This was an English folk tale collected by
J.O. Halliwell in 1853 and printed in 1890.
It is similar to a Grimm's fairy tale, *The Wolf
and the Seven Little Kids* and an earlier
English tale *The History of the Celebrated
Nanny Goose* printed in 1813, in which
three goslings try to foil the fox with
their three houses of straw, furze (or twigs)
and bricks.

In 1933 *The Three Little Pigs* was made
into a very successful Disney cartoon and
the song "Who's Afraid of the Big Bad Wolf?"
became a rallying cry in America, where the
wolf came to be seen as a symbol
of the Depression.